Uh-oh!

The witch picked up the mortar and looked at the powder. "Boy, will they be in for a surprise in the forest," she said with a chuckle. "Heeheehee."

"How do you mean?" asked the hare.

"There will be lots of white walnuts lying around in the forest in the next few days, heeheehee."

The hare looked at her uncertainly. "What are you going to change, then?"

"Whatever. The animals, if they're a bother."

"The an . . . the animals . . . ," the hare stammered.

"Yes! Then they'll remember who's boss here in the forest."

"But—but—how are you going to turn them back again?"

The witch shrugged. "I don't know. But maybe I'll figure that out some day."

The hare swallowed.

"A very pleasant visit to an idyllic community, where the animals, each with its own distinct personality, look out for each other, and even the wicked witch is really only naughty." —*Booklist*

OTHER PUFFIN BOOKS YOU MAY ENJOY

THE
WICKED WITCH
Is at It Again

Hanna Kraan

illustrations by
Annemarie van Haeringen

Translation by
Wanda Boeke

PUFFIN BOOKS

PUFFIN BOOKS

Published by the Penguin Group

Penguin Putnam Inc., 375 Hudson Street, New York, New York 10014, U.S.A.

Penguin Books Ltd, 27 Wrights Lane, London W8 5TZ, England

Penguin Books Australia Ltd, Ringwood, Victoria, Australia

Penguin Books Canada Ltd, 10 Alcorn Avenue, Toronto, Ontario, Canada M4V 3B2

Penguin Books (N.Z.) Ltd, 182-190 Wairau Road, Auckland 10, New Zealand

Penguin Books Ltd, Registered Offices: Harmondsworth, Middlesex, England

Originally published in the Netherlands under the title *De bose heks is weer bezig!*
First published in the United States of America by Front Street Books, 1997
Published by Puffin Books,
a member of Penguin Putnam Books for Young Readers, 1998

1 3 5 7 9 10 8 6 4 2

LIBRARY OF CONGRESS CATALOGING-IN-PUBLICATION DATA
Kraan, Hannah.
[Boze heks is weer bezig. English]
The wicked witch is at it again! / Hannah Kraan ; illustrated by Annemarie van
Haeringen; translated by Wanda Boeke. p. cm.
Summary: The continuing adventures of a not-quite-so-wicked witch who lives in
the forest with an owl, a hare, and a hedgehog.
ISBN 0-14-130078-7 (pbk.)
[1. Witches—Fiction. 2. Forest animals—Fiction.] I. Haeringen, Annemarie van,
ill. II. Boeke, Wanda. III. Title.
[PZ7.K857Wi 1998] [Fic]—dc21 98-16334 CIP AC

Printed in the United States of America

CONTENTS

THE WICKED WITCH IS BORED

The wicked witch sat in her chair and yawned. Well, what was she going to do today? Bake a cake? No, she didn't feel like doing that. Make berry juice, knit a scarf . . . she didn't feel like doing that, either. The witch sighed. She didn't feel like doing anything, really. She was bored. Funny, she never used to get bored. She was always casting spells, or thinking of little ways to give the animals a hard time . . .

"I've been too good lately," the witch said out loud. "And being good is boring."

She got up and shambled over to the closet. "Might as well clean the closet. I don't feel like doing that, either, but it has to be done sometime."

She opened the closet door and began clearing off a shelf.

But what was that? Under the towels and sheets lay a big, thick book.

"My book of magic spells!" exclaimed the witch. "That's right—I put it away in a good place. My good old book of spells!"

Carefully she took the book out of the closet and laid it on the table. She opened it and began turning the pages. "Disappearing water, forgetting powder . . . I used to make that all the time. Turning animals into pine cones . . . I don't need a book to do that, I can easily do it without." She flipped through the book some more.

"Aha, now we're getting to the difficult recipes. Dizzying potion, gibberish water, quacking powder . . . I never made any of those. They're so complicated and it's easy for things to go wrong. But now I've got plenty of time," murmured the witch. "Let's see. Dizzying potion. What do I need to make that?"

The hare and the hedgehog were sitting in the sun, bored and out of sorts.

"Shall we go for a run?" asked the hare.

"No," said the hedgehog.

"Play a game, hide-and-seek, throw chestnuts?"

"No."

"Or do something useful, help somebody or make something?"

"No."

"What do you want to do, then?"

"I don't want to do anything. I'm bored."

The hare thought for a moment. "I'm bored, too, I think. That's funny. I never used to be."

They heard an "Oo-hoo!" way above their heads.

The hare and the hedgehog looked up. It was the owl, flying quickly down.

"That's where you two are," he said. "I've been looking all over for you."

"What's going on?" the hare asked.

"The wicked witch is up to something," said the owl. "She's making a magic potion."

"Are you sure?" asked the hare. "She hasn't done that for a long time."

"She doesn't anymore, that's right," said the hedgehog. "What makes you think she's making one *now*?"

"I was flying over her cabin and this awful-smelling smoke was coming out of the chimney, just like it used to."

The hedgehog yawned. "I'm sure she let something burn. Apple pie, probably. Or pancakes."

"No, no, no!" said the owl impatiently. "That smells different. But come have a look, if you don't believe me."

The hare got up. "We're going to look into this," he said to the hedgehog. "Come on, then you won't have to be bored anymore."

Reluctantly the hedgehog got up and trudged after the others.

"There!" the owl said, pointing, when they had reached the witch's cabin. "Greenish-purple smoke."

"Funny," said the hare. He sniffed. "Phew! That isn't apple pie. Not even burned apple pie."

The hedgehog also sniffed. "Burned pancakes," he said.

The hare and the owl weren't listening to him. Quietly they went up to the little window and looked inside. The wicked witch was stirring something in a big cauldron. From time to time she went over to the table and looked at a thick book.

"She really is making a magic potion," the hare

whispered.

"Let me see," said the hedgehog. He pushed the others aside, stood on the tips of his toes, and looked through the window. "I don't see the witch at all!"

"Ooyooyooy!" the animals heard close at hand. They jumped back.

The wicked witch was standing in her doorway. "I thought I saw something at the window! What are you spying on? Are you planning to steal something?"

"No, no," stammered the owl. "But there was a really strange smell and we thought—"

"—that your pancakes had burned!" the hedgehog exclaimed.

The witch looked at him with suspicion. Then she chuckled. "You smelled right," she said. "The pancakes did burn."

"Can we do anything?" the hare asked.

"No," said the witch brusquely. "And now, off with you. I have to get back to work. Make a new batch of pancakes, heeheehee." She closed the door.

"Now, you see? She *was* making pancakes," said the hedgehog.

The hare shook his head and whispered, "Didn't you see that big, round cauldron? You can't fry pancakes in there. She just said that to get rid of us."

"Oh, no!" exclaimed the hedgehog. "That's mean!"

"Shhh!" whispered the hare. "Come on." He pulled the others over to a massive beech tree. "There. If we sit behind this tree, she won't be able to see us."

"What are you going to do?" asked the owl.

"Make that potion harmless. I don't know how, yet, but . . ."

The door of the cabin opened. The witch stepped outside with a basket over her arm. Mumbling to herself, she shambled right past the beech tree. The animals held their breath.

"Gagroot," the witch mumbled. "And adder-grass. Not too much and not too little. Exactly what the recipe says, otherwise it won't work."

She disappeared into the forest.

"Come on," said the hare. "This is our chance. And take something in with you." He picked up some leaves.

"Why?" asked the owl.

"You heard what she said. The magic potion will work only if it's made exactly according to the recipe. So if we throw other things into it, it won't work anymore."

"Of course!" exclaimed the owl. "Very clever!" He quickly picked a couple of mushrooms. The hedgehog gathered a handful of beechnuts. Together the three snuck into the cabin.

The owl looked at the magic book. "Dizzying potion," he said. "You see?"

"Hurry up," said the hare. "She could come back any minute."

He threw the leaves into the cauldron. The owl added the mushrooms and the hedgehog sprinkled the beechnuts over the rim. The potion in the cauldron began to foam and fizzle.

"Add something else," the hare ordered. "It doesn't matter what."

"A spoonful of sugar," said the hedgehog. "And her slippers. Here."

"That's it," said the hare. "Now it'll—"

"Ooyooyooy!" a voice threatened from the doorway. "What are you doing here?"

Pale with fear, the animals looked around. There stood the witch with her basket.

"So, you are stealing? I thought so. I'll get you!"

"We only came in to—" whispered the owl.

"—to ask if we could have a pancake," said the hare quickly.

"But you aren't making pancakes at all!" the hedgehog exclaimed. "You only said that to get rid of us. But I had it figured out right away!"

"Stand still, all three of you," said the witch. "Since you're here anyway, I might as well see if my dizzying potion turned out."

She went over to the cauldron, tossed in a few plants from her basket, and stirred with a big wooden spoon. The hare nudged the others and pointed toward the door. They started to tiptoe away.

"Stay here!" cried the witch. In a flash she had scooped a spoonful of magic potion into a pitcher of water and emptied the pitcher over the owl.

The hare and the hedgehog stood motionless and stared anxiously at the owl.

The owl felt himself get dizzy for just an instant. He slowly spun around once, then it was over. He shook the water from his feathers and winked.

Relieved, the hare and the hedgehog started to laugh.

"Your dizzying stuff jolly well doesn't work!" the hedgehog exclaimed.

"Better luck next time," said the hare.

The witch looked at the owl in dismay. "How can that be?" she muttered. "Why aren't you spinning around in circles?"

She began wildly stirring the potion. Suddenly she stopped.

"It would seem there are mushrooms in it," she said in surprise. "And leaves!"

"And a spoonful of sugar," said the hedgehog.

"You messed up my dizzying potion!"

The hedgehog opened the door. "If you're looking for your slippers . . . ," he said over his shoulder.

The witch looked around. "Where are my slippers?"

"You'll find them when you throw that potion away," giggled the hedgehog as he leaped outside. The hare and the owl ran after him.

"You'll pay for this!" shrieked the witch. "I'll get you! Ooyooyooy!" Waving her wooden spoon, she hurried outside, into the forest.

From behind the big beech tree the hare and the owl and the hedgehog followed her with their eyes.

"Luckily that ended well," said the hare.

The owl wiped the last drop of water from his wing and sighed. "Yes, but now that the witch is doing magic again, our peace and quiet will be gone."

"Our boredom, too," said the hare.

"I'm never bored," said the hedgehog. "Do you want to come over to my house? I'm going to make some pancakes!"

Leaning into the wind, the hare and the owl and the hedgehog walked through the forest.

"What a wind," said the owl breathlessly.

The hare stuck his paw in the air. "A stiff breeze out of the southwest," he said.

"He calls that a stiff breeze," the hedgehog grumbled. "It's a storm! And not just a little one."

The wind whistled through the trees. The animals had to brace themselves to stay on their feet.

"We'd better find cover," panted the hare. "There, behind that little hill. Then we'll be out of the wind."

With difficulty they reached the hillock. The hedgehog sprawled on the ground. "Pfff . . ."

"We'll be fine here," said the hare. "Just stay down."

"It's blowing harder and harder," said the owl. "Just listen to that wind howl."

They heard an eerie ooyooyooy sound.

The hedgehog sat up with a start. "I hear the wicked witch!"

"That's just the wind," the hare explained. "The wind in the tree branches."

Ooyooyooy . . . It was closer now.

"There!" the hedgehog squeaked, pointing up at the sky. "Didn't I tell you? It is the wicked witch."

Startled, the hare and the owl looked up.

It was the wicked witch. She was flying their way full speed on her broom. She zoomed over

the hillock, made a loop and came back toward them.

"Ooyooyooy!" she sang out. "Now, this is real weather for witches! Go ahead, let it storm."

"Ma'am, watch out!" exclaimed the hare. "You'll blow off your broom!"

"Of course not! Flying is wonderful in a storm. I'll turn you all into flies, then you can fly, too, heeheehee!"

"No!" cried the hedgehog. "Don't! I'm leaving!" And he started to run.

The hare and the owl followed him as quickly as they could, but it wasn't easy against the wind. And there was the witch again. "Ooyooyooy!"

"Help, help," spluttered the owl.

"Keep running," gasped the hare.

The hedgehog stood still. He turned around, shook his fist at the witch, and shouted, "I wish you'd blow away! Far, far away!"

"Impudent prickly creature!" shrieked the witch. "How dare you! I'll turn you into a—"

HOOY!!!

There was such a blast of wind that the hedgehog couldn't stay on his feet. He was knocked over and rolled on the ground until he came to a stop against a bush. Dizzily he looked around. There were the hare and the owl. They were hanging on to a tree and gazing wide-eyed at the sky. The hedgehog also looked up. There was nothing to be seen.

Where had the wicked witch gone?

The hedgehog shrugged his shoulders. "Must have gone home to eat." He scrambled to his feet. "Did you see me fall?"

"The witch blew away," said the hare, upset.

"I was blown slam-bam to the ground," said the hedgehog.

"Where could she be?" the owl asked with concern.

"Hey!" shouted the hedgehog. "I could have broken something! I could have died!"

"We have to go look for her," said the hare. "Are you guys coming?"

"Not me," said the hedgehog angrily. "I'm going home. I have to have some quiet after everything I've just been through."

"But it's your fault," said the owl reproachfully.

"My fault? Her own fault! Who would go out and sit on a broom in a storm?"

"You wanted her to blow away."

The hedgehog turned pale. "But . . . but . . . I didn't do anything. It was the wind . . ."

"Maybe she fell down somewhere. Maybe she's hurt."

"Are you guys coming or not?" the hare asked impatiently.

The owl turned around and followed the hare.

The hedgehog watched them go. "I might have gotten hurt, too," he grumbled. "But nobody cares about that." He heaved a sigh and trotted after them.

"Luckily it isn't blowing so hard anymore," said the hare. "We should go that way, she was blown over there."

"I'll go take a look," said the owl, ready to fly off.

The hare held him back. "I'll go take a look. Otherwise you'll be blown away, too. One's bad enough."

"Two's bad enough," said the hedgehog.

The hare ran over to the little hill behind which they had taken cover. He ran to the top, shaded his eyes with his paw, and peered into the distance.

"I see her!" he exclaimed. "She's in a fallen tree. Come on!"

They had to walk a long way, but finally they reached a large tree that lay straight across the path. The witch, looking pale, was sitting in the branches.

"We've come to rescue you!" called the hare. "Did you hurt yourself, ma'am?"

"No," said the witch in a shaky voice. "I landed right in the branches. But my dress is snagged."

Carefully the animals freed the witch from the branches.

"There we go," said the hare. "Luckily that ended well. We'll bring you home."

"My broom," mumbled the witch. "Where did my broom go?"

"There it is." The owl pointed. "We'll carry it for you."

"No, just give it here. Then I can lean on it."

Using her broom as a cane, the witch shuffled home. The hare and the owl walked beside her and told her how worried they had been. The hedgehog followed behind looking glum.

"I fell, too," he mulled. "Slam-bam to the ground. But nobody cares about me."

When they got to the witch's little cabin, the hare turned around. "Are you coming? We're going to have some chocolate milk at the witch's."

The hedgehog nodded and went in with them.

The owl brought the witch to her chair. "Why don't you just sit down. We'll take care of the chocolate milk."

"I'm going to just sit down, too," said the hedgehog. "I'm all confused and black-and-blue all over."

"How come?" asked the witch.

"I fell down," said the hedgehog in a little voice. "The wind went hooy! and I was blown down slam-bam."

"Poor hedgehog," said the witch. "Come, I'm sure I have a little herbal drink for you, for the fright."

"No, no, don't bother," the hedgehog said quickly. "I'm feeling better already."

The hare winked. "The hedgehog can take a few knocks," he said. "He's very brave."

"He never complains," said the owl. "Never!"

The hedgehog nodded proudly.

"Here's some chocolate milk," said the hare. "That's good for a fright, too."

With his eyes closed, the hedgehog drank his chocolate milk. Then he licked his lips, smiled at the witch, and said, "I didn't mean it, you know, what I said this morning."

The witch looked at him questioningly. "And what was it again you said this morning?"

The hare gave the hedgehog a sharp nudge and said loudly, "From the sound of it, the wind has died down completely."

The owl plucked nervously at the tablecloth.

"What was it you said?" the witch asked again.

"That—that I wanted you to blow away . . . ," stammered the hedgehog.

"That's right!" shrieked the witch. "I'd forgotten all about that. Impertinent creature that you are! I'll turn you into a woolly bear!" She leaped to her feet.

The hedgehog ran for the door and disappeared outside as quickly as he could. The witch wanted to go after him, but the hare held her back.

"We should be getting on our way, too," he said.

"Thank you for the chocolate milk," said the owl politely.

And off they went, into the forest.

In the open place in the middle of the forest they stood still.

"Ooyooyooy!" they could hear in the distance.

"There she goes, whooping it up again," said the owl, shaking his head.

The hare smiled. "Luckily she's none the worse for wear," he said.

THE HARE DRAWS A PICTURE

The hare had his sketchbook tucked under his arm, his pencils in his hand, as he looked around thoughtfully.

Well, what should he draw?

There! Two yellow butterflies were fluttering after each other.

"That'll be a beautiful drawing," murmured the hare. He sat down and opened up his sketchbook.

But the butterflies fluttered up and down and over and up again.

"Hey!" shouted the hare. "Can't you guys stay in one place for just a second? For just one second?"

The butterflies didn't even hear him. They fluttered higher and higher and then they were gone.

The hare sighed. He closed his sketchbook and got up.

A little farther on, six young rabbits were leaping around and doing somersaults. The hare began to sketch quickly, but then he shook his head.

"I can't draw that quickly," he grumbled.

The young rabbits hopped up, jostling one another, and gathered around him.

"What are you doing?"

"What's it going to be?"

"Can we do it, too?"

"I'm drawing all of you," the hare explained.

The young rabbits looked at one another and started giggling.

"That isn't what it looks like at all!" the rudest one exclaimed. "It's just a couple of hen scratches."

"That's because you all move too much," said the hare sternly. "Go and sit down quietly for a while. Like that. And stay like that, so I can make a nice drawing."

The young rabbits sat quietly for a moment. Then the first one shoved the second one. The second one punched back, the third one rolled over, and there they all were again, horsing around and doing somersaults.

"Sit still!" cried the hare.

But the young rabbits thumbed their noses at him and went noisily on their way.

"Bah," said the hare. "This isn't going to work. And it's such nice weather for drawing."

He picked up his things and walked on. He passed the wicked witch's little cabin. He wanted to walk on quickly, but suddenly he stopped.

"Beautiful, that sunlight on the roof," he murmured. "And those flowers on the side and the dark trees in back . . ."

He sat down, took another good look, and set to work.

He was so busy concentrating that he didn't notice there was someone coming.

"What are you doing?" he heard suddenly, right behind his back.

The hare dropped his pencil and looked around. The hedgehog was giving the sketchbook a dirty look.

"The wicked witch's cabin," said the hedgehog. "Can't you find something nicer?"

"It is nice, with that sunlight on it," said the hare impatiently. "And at least it stands still. And you shouldn't talk to me, because I want to work."

"I'm going, I'm going," said the hedgehog, insulted. "But if I were you, I'd be careful. If the witch comes out . . ."

They heard creaking.

The door of the witch's cabin opened and the wicked witch came outside.

"What are you doing over there? You have no business here. Go away!"

"I'm drawing your house, ma'am," said the

hare. "Look."

He held up his sketchbook.

"Worthless doodling! Go scribble somewhere else. I don't want any messing around or any spying right outside my door."

"I'm not doing anything and I'm not spying," said the hedgehog indignantly. "I wouldn't even want a drawing of your caved-in old house!"

"Caved-in!" shouted the witch. "My house isn't caved in! I'll cave in your spines!" She stepped forward threateningly. "I'll make you vanish! I'll turn you into a long-legged mosquito!"

The hedgehog ducked out of sight behind the hare. "Stop her!" he squeaked.

The hare took a deep breath. "Ma'am, would you like me to make a nice drawing of you?"

The witch stood still. "Of me?"

"Yes! I almost finished your house. If you would sit over by the door, I'll draw you in."

The witch blushed. She walked back toward the door. "Right about here?"

"A little to the side. Yes, that's it. Hedgehog, go sit over there, too."

"Are you out of your mind?" whispered the hedgehog. "Sure, next to the wicked witch. Then you'll end up with a nice drawing of a long-legged mosquito."

"I don't want that prickly creature in my drawing," snapped the witch.

"But it'll look nicer if he's in it," the hare explained as he pushed the hedgehog forward.

"That'll create depth."

"Oh, depth," said the witch. "You should have said that in the first place."

The hare picked up his pencil from the ground and feverishly started to draw. The wicked witch sat motionless in front of the door. With a frozen smile she stared straight ahead.

The hedgehog strolled back and forth. He sniffed at flowers and waved at every bird that flew by.

"Sit still!" said the hare.

"I am sitting still," said the hedgehog. "But it's taking so long." He plucked a blade of grass and waved it at the wicked witch.

The witch looked straight ahead.

The hedgehog got a little closer and tickled the witch under her nose with the blade of grass.

"Ha . . . hachee!" sneezed the witch. "Quit that! Hachoo!"

The hedgehog shook with laughter.

"Watch out, you," the witch threatened between her teeth. "As soon as I can move again, I'll . . ."

"Done!" exclaimed the hare.

The witch jumped to her feet. The hedgehog ran away, but the witch was paying no attention to him. She went right over to the hare and looked at the drawing.

"Oooh . . . ," she said admiringly. "How clever! That's me, to a tee."

"Yes, it turned out pretty well," said the hare

and ran his paw over his whiskers, pleased.

Out of curiosity, the hedgehog drew near. "What's that on the side there? A clump of grass?"

"No . . . ," said the hare. "That's you."

The hedgehog looked at him indignantly.

"You kept moving!" said the hare.

The witch started to scream with laughter. "Heehahoo! A clump of grass! That's what you get, heehahoo!"

"It's no laughing matter," said the hedgehog irritably. "And I don't look like a clump of grass."

The hare sighed. "It's very hard to draw a hedgehog . . ."

"That's true," said the hedgehog. "Much harder than a witch. Drawing a witch, anybody can do that."

"You think so?" exclaimed the witch. "Always you! I'll turn you into a clump of grass! Nobody will be able to tell the difference anyway, heeheehee."

"Here you are, ma'am," said the hare. "You may have the drawing."

"Really?" exclaimed the witch happily. She carefully reached for the drawing. "Thank you very much! I'm going to hang it up right away."

She turned around and went inside her cabin.

The hedgehog tugged at the hare's arm. "Give me your sketchbook for a second. And your pencils."

The hare slid the sketchbook over to him. "What are you going to do?"

"I'm going to show you how to draw a hedge-hog. You can't look!"

The hare sat down with his back to the hedge-hog. He hummed a tune and then another tune. After the seventh tune he asked, "Not working out?"

"It *is* working out," said the hedgehog. "It's working out very well, in fact."

"May I look?"

"Almost!" said the hedgehog. He tore the sheet of paper out of the sketchbook and crumpled it up.

The hare looked around in surprise.

The hedgehog kicked the wad far into the forest. "It really is very hard to draw a hedgehog," he said with a sigh.

THROWING CHESTNUTS

Singing loudly, the hedgehog walked through the forest.

> "As long as a hedgehog has his spines
> there is nothing for him to fear.
> As long as a hedgehog has—Ow!"

Something hard had just hit him on the head.
The hedgehog stood still and carefully felt his

head. Ouch! He looked down. In front of his feet lay a large chestnut. The hedgehog picked it up. Suddenly he jumped to the side. Another chestnut whizzed past him and rolled onto the ground beside him.

"They're throwing chestnuts at me!" said the hedgehog indignantly. "Who would do a thing like that?"

"I won!" he heard in the distance.

"The hare," said the hedgehog. "That was the hare's voice. I'll go see."

He walked on quickly. When he reached the

open place in the middle of the forest, he saw the hare and the blackbird. They were standing next to each other. At their feet lay a pile of chestnuts.

"Now me again," said the blackbird. He picked up a chestnut and was about to throw it.

"Hey!" exclaimed the hedgehog. "Whoa!"

"Aha, the hedgehog," said the hare. "Do you want to join us?"

"Why are you holding on to your head?" the blackbird asked.

"I was hit on the head by a chestnut," complained the hedgehog.

The hare slapped his paw over his mouth.

"I was just walking along, walking along and singing, and suddenly I felt something hard and then everything went black in front of my eyes."

"How terrible," said the hare unhappily. "We were seeing who could throw the farthest and I won."

"I must have been unconscious for half an hour," said the hedgehog plaintively.

The hare and the blackbird looked at each other. "Half an hour ago we weren't even here," said the hare. "We just started."

"Then it was a little shorter," said the hedgehog quickly. "When you're unconscious, you have no concept of time."

"You weren't unconscious at all," exclaimed the blackbird. "Faker!"

"I could have been unconscious," said the hedgehog. "It hit me hard."

"Where were you, exactly, when it happened?" asked the hare.

"Just past the fallen tree."

"All the way over there!" exclaimed the hare. "I threw that far. Boy!"

"Pooh," said the hedgehog. "I can throw way farther. Way, way farther. Just watch."

"Me first," said the blackbird. He threw. The chestnut disappeared among the trees.

"Well, that wasn't very far," said the hedgehog. "That's nothing."

"You do it better, then," said the blackbird.

The hedgehog swung his arm back and threw as hard as he could. The chestnut flew up and then fell straight down, not even three feet away from the hedgehog. The blackbird chuckled.

"How can that be?" said the hedgehog, taken aback. "Another try, the first time doesn't count." He threw another chestnut, but that one also fell to the ground in a feeble arc.

"You have to throw well to the front," said the hare. "See, like this."

"I know how I'm supposed to throw," the hedgehog said irritably.

"Of course you do have to have some muscle," said the blackbird.

"I have muscle!" exclaimed the hedgehog. "But it's against the wind."

"Oh, yeah?" the blackbird intoned, and he threw a chestnut far away.

The hedgehog threw another chestnut. It

plopped to the ground nearby.

The blackbird started to laugh jeeringly.

Beaten, the hedgehog sat down.

The hare shook his head and said softly, "There's something that doesn't make sense here . . ."

"He just can't throw," said the blackbird.

"I can too!" exclaimed the hedgehog, jumping to his feet. "And better than you!"

"You call that better? You—"

"Shhh!" said the hare. "Quiet a second, you guys. I thought I heard something."

They all listened. "Heeheehee," they heard.

The hare nodded. "Too bad I didn't think of that sooner. The wicked witch. I'm sure she'll know something more about it."

"The witch!" exclaimed the hedgehog. "Of course! She made me lose!" He looked around. "Where are you? Come out!"

The witch came out from behind a tree and ambled up with a grin on her face.

The hedgehog hopped up and down in a rage. "It's all your fault!" he shouted. "You were hexing my chestnuts to the ground!"

"It was only a joke," the witch chuckled. "You were boasting so much."

"A joke! I'll get you one of these days, you and your jokes! I'll . . ."

"Here," said the hare as he shoved a chestnut into the hedgehog's hand. "Try it now."

The hedgehog fixed the wicked witch with a

stare. "No magic!" he said.

He let fly. With a whoosh the chestnut flew off into the forest.

The hare and the blackbird and the witch clapped.

The hedgehog turned around proudly. "You see? I can throw. I throw the farthest of anybody."

"Whoa," said the blackbird. "That we still have to see." He also threw.

"Now me," said the hare.

"May I try, too?" asked the witch. The hare gave her a chestnut. The witch threw, but the chestnut didn't go very far.

"Hahaha!" cried the hedgehog and the blackbird. "The witch can't do it at all! Haha!"

The witch looked around irritably. "Stop it or I'll hex you orange!"

The hedgehog and the blackbird shut their mouths in fear.

"That's what I thought," muttered the witch. "Rude, uncouth oafs!" She shuffled off into the forest.

"You shouldn't have laughed at her," said the hare.

"She laughed at me," grumbled the hedgehog.

"She doesn't mean it in a bad way," said the hare. "At least, not all the time. But I'm starting to feel hungry. Do you guys want to eat at my house?"

"Sure," said the blackbird.

"In a little while," said the hedgehog. "Let's

wait for a moment." He picked up a chestnut and flung it into the forest.

"Very good! Nice and far!" exclaimed the hare and the blackbird.

Suddenly they could hear the thud of footsteps, and there was the wicked witch, running across the open space in the forest.

"I was hit on the head by a chestnut!" she shrieked. "On top of my hat! Who did that?"

The hedgehog grabbed the hare and the blackbird. "On second thought, let's go eat now," he said and started to run.

THE HARE WANTS TO HELP

The door to the witch's cabin was wide open. The wicked witch was sitting on the threshold with the book of magic spells on her lap. Deep in thought, she stared off into the distance. The hare came running by.

"Good morning!" he called. "Nice weather today."

The witch didn't respond. She sighed and shook her head.

Hesitantly the hare walked back. "What's wrong?" he asked.

"It needs something else," the witch said pensively. "But what?"

"What needs something else?"

The witch pointed at her book. "I'm making a magic powder. But part of the page was torn off and now I don't know what else to add. I've already tried everything, but it won't work."

"What's the powder for?" the hare asked cautiously.

"To conjure up a white walnut."

"A white walnut? How exciting. May I help?"

"Fine by me," said the witch. "Maybe you can think of what should be added."

The hare looked around. "Stinging nettles?"

"Nettles . . . ," said the witch and she stood up. "That might very well be. Come on in."

The hare followed the witch inside. On the

table was a big mortar filled with powder. The witch took a jam jar full of dried leaves out of the cupboard and shook the contents out into the mortar. She pounded the leaves to powder, then slid the mortar over to the hare.

"Mix it well," she said.

The hare stirred energetically. "Green-brown powder," he said. "How can you possibly make a white walnut from that?"

"Just wait," said the witch. "We're going to try it right away."

She placed a stone in the middle of the table. Then she took a handful of powder, sprinkled it over the stone, and mumbled a lot of magic words.

The hare waited with bated breath.

Nothing happened.

"Wrong again," sighed the witch.

The hare looked at the cupboard. "Maybe some salt?" he asked. "Or pepper? Flour?"

"Flour!" exclaimed the witch. "That's it!"

She took a spoonful of flour from the cupboard and sprinkled it into the mortar.

"I'll stir," said the hare.

Again the witch took some powder, sprinkled it over the stone, and mumbled her magic words.

The stone slowly began to change. It became rounder and lighter and suddenly there was a white walnut lying on the table.

With big eyes the hare watched. "It's working!" he exclaimed. "Hurrah!"

"That was it!" crowed the witch. "Flour! I should have thought of that myself."

She took the hare by the arm, and together they danced around the table.

Then the witch flopped into a chair and panted, "You've got a talent for magic!"

The hare stroked his whiskers. "It was just a guess," he said modestly.

The witch picked up the mortar and looked at the powder. "Boy, will they be in for a surprise in the forest," she said with a chuckle. "Heeheehee."

"How do you mean?" asked the hare.

"There will be lots of white walnuts lying around in the forest in the next few days, heeheehee."

The hare looked at her uncertainly. "What are you going to change, then?"

"Whatever. The animals, if they're a bother."

"The an . . . the animals . . . ," the hare stammered.

"Yes! Then they'll remember who's boss here in the forest."

"But—but—how are you going to turn them back again?"

The witch shrugged. "I don't know. But maybe I'll figure that out some day. And then you can help again!"

The hare swallowed. "Fine," he said. "Thank you very much. But I have to go now. Good-bye!"

"Good-bye, hare. And thanks again for your help."

With his head bowed, the hare walked home.

"Thanks again for your help," he repeated softly. "What have I done! I helped the witch so she could hurt the animals . . ."

He sat down outside the door to his house.

The owl flew by slowly. When he saw the hare, he quickly flew down.

"What's wrong?" he asked, concerned.

"Something terrible," said the hare. "The witch has a magic powder that can turn us all into white walnuts."

"White walnuts? But that's impossible. Are you sure?"

"Yes," whispered the hare. "Because I helped make the powder."

"You?"

"Yes . . . ," sighed the hare, and he told of how he had helped the witch. "So it's all my fault," he said dully.

The owl patted him on the shoulder. "There wasn't any way for you to know that. But she just isn't to be trusted."

"I only wanted to help," said the hare sadly.

A heavy silence fell.

The owl got up. "I might as well go and warn the others. Maybe it won't be so bad after all."

He flew away.

The hare blinked his eyes. "I hope so," he murmured.

He went inside and sat down at the table. Thinking, he drummed on a book that was lying

in the middle of the table.

"I have to make that powder harmless," he brooded. "But if she still knows what's in it, she can easily make some more . . ."

There was a knock at the door, and it swung open right away.

The wicked witch came in holding the mortar. "You have to help out again for a minute," she said. "It isn't quite right yet."

"It isn't?" the hare asked hopefully.

"No," said the witch. "Just look."

She took a handful of powder, sprinkled it over the book, and mumbled some magic words.

The book became smaller and rounder and whiter, and on the table lay a white walnut.

The hare trembled. "Uh-oh, uh-oh . . . ," he said softly.

"And now, pay attention," said the witch. "Just look what happens."

The hare looked carefully at the walnut. At first nothing happened. But after a while the walnut became flatter and longer and broader and very slowly a book reappeared.

"Hurrah!" exclaimed the hare.

The witch looked at him indignantly.

"I was afraid I'd lost my book," the hare said quickly. "And I hadn't finished it yet."

"Oh, that's why," said the witch. "But did you see that? After a couple of minutes the powder's effect is gone. We still did something wrong."

The hare thought hard. "I think I know what it is," he said.

"Yes?" the witch asked greedily. "How smart! I told you you had a talent for magic."

The hare picked up the mortar. "It just has to be stirred even better."

He went over to the door. "I'll go stir it outside. Otherwise the powder will be all over the room."

The witch nodded.

The hare took a couple of steps outside, turned the mortar over, and blew as hard as he could. A cloud of powder disappeared among the trees.

"Help!" cried the hare. "Oh, how terrible! Come quick!"

"What's going on, what's going on?" exclaimed the witch as she ran outside.

The hare showed her the empty mortar. "All of a sudden there was this gust of wind, a really strong gust, and everything was gone."

"My powder!" moaned the witch. "All that work for nothing! Idiot!"

"I'm really very sorry," said the hare with a sad look on his face. When the witch wasn't looking, he quickly blew the very last of the powder out of the mortar.

"Idiot!" The witch stamped her foot angrily. "It's only because you helped me, otherwise . . ."

"It happened because of that gust of wind," said the hare. "And the powder didn't work very well anyway."

"It only worked for a little while," said the witch with a sigh. "And I can't remember what all I put in there. All that work for nothing!"

She snatched the mortar away from the hare and stomped off to her house.

The hare made a little leap for joy. Then he ran as fast as he could to the tree where the owl lived.

"Owl! Owl! Come out!"

The owl stuck his head through the leaves.

"The powder is gone! At first it worked, but not after that, and then I blew it away."

The owl thought for a moment. "So it's gone?" he asked.

"Yes!" exclaimed the hare. "The walnut turned back into a book, and when I went outside to stir, I blew it all away!"

The owl spread his wings and floated down.

"If I understand this correctly, we can go tell the others that the danger is past," he said. "And after that you'll have to explain it to me again, slowly."

THE WITCH'S BROOM

The hedgehog sprinted through the forest. He ran as close as he could to the trees, and from time to time he looked up fearfully.

The wicked witch had thought up something new. For a couple of days already she had been flying over the forest every morning, throwing puffballs around. The hedgehog had just spent a long time pulling the puffballs off his spines.

He reached the sand-drift. Here he had to cross an open space. As fast as he could, he started running to the other side. But halfway, his foot got caught on something and there he lay, sprawled out in the sand. "Ow!"

He got up again and looked at what he had tripped over.

Half covered by sand lay a long stick.

"Hey . . . ," said the hedgehog. He pulled at the stick. "It's a broom. The witch's broom!"

The hedgehog quickly looked around. There was nobody to be seen. He dragged the broom over to the trees.

"A real witch's broom," he whispered excitedly. "But then the witch can't be very far away. Let's first find a safe spot."

He thought for a moment. "At home, under my bed!"

He quickly walked on, dragging the broom behind him.

But it wasn't all that easy. The broom was big and heavy and the hedgehog was getting hotter and hotter.

All of a sudden a shadow fell across the path.

"Help! The witch!" squeaked the hedgehog. He let go of the broom and hid behind a tree.

But it wasn't the witch. It was the owl, alighting on the path.

The hedgehog reappeared. "Oh, it's only you," he said with relief. "I thought it was the witch."

"How did you get that broom?" asked the owl.

"Found it. Over there, by the sand-drift."

"Where are you taking it?"

"To the witch, of course."

The owl shook his head. "The witch's cabin is that way," he said. "This is the way to your own

house."

The hedgehog dropped his eyes. Then he shrugged and said, "If I bring it back to the witch, she'll just start throwing puffballs again. I'm jolly well going to keep it."

"Oh, don't do that," said the owl nervously. "That will only cause trouble. When the witch realizes that you stole her broom—"

"Not stole. Found."

"—you can be sure she will come take revenge. She's probably out already looking for it at this very moment."

The hedgehog looked behind himself fearfully.

"So, just come along with me," said the owl. "We'll bring it back together."

The hedgehog heaved a sigh. "Oh, all right,"

he muttered.

Together they carried the broom to the witch's cabin.

The owl knocked at the door. The witch opened it. "What is it?" she asked in a surly tone.

"We have something for you," said the owl.

"My broom!" exclaimed the witch. "How did you two get hold of it?"

"I found it just now," said the hedgehog. "By the sand-drift."

"How can that be?" said the witch. "That's where I left it this morning when I went to look for puffballs. But when I got back, it was gone. I looked everywhere."

"The wind covered it with sand," the hedgehog explained. "I tripped over it." He looked at the owl. "And of course I immediately came to return it."

The owl nodded. "Immediately! And I helped carry it."

"How good of you," the witch said, pleased. "Would you like some blackberry juice? I'll conjure up a cake to go with it."

"Sure!" said the owl. "Blackberry juice and cake, how delicious."

"I'm not hungry," said the hedgehog, with a quick glance at the witch. "I'll guard the broom."

"Up to you," said the witch, and she went inside.

"Oh, come on," whispered the owl.

"No," the hedgehog whispered back. "Once she tied my spines in knots and just this morning she was throwing puffballs at me. I'm staying outside. But I'll wait for you."

The owl hesitated. Then he followed the witch indoors. The door closed behind him.

The hedgehog waited for a moment. From inside the cabin came the sound of conversation and the clinking of glasses. The hedgehog tiptoed over to the broom. Carefully he mounted it. Nothing happened.

The hedgehog grasped the handle and hopped, broom and all. "This isn't how it works," he muttered. He stood up and lifted the broom high into the air. "Not this way, either."

He lay the broom on the ground, sat on top of it again, and in a deep voice said, "Fly!"

The broom moved. The hedgehog grabbed hold of the handle and—hup!—he slowly rose into the air. "It's working!" whispered the hedgehog.

The broom climbed higher and higher. He was already above the witch's cabin, above the trees . . .

"Not so high!" squeaked the hedgehog. The broom dropped a little.

The hedgehog leaned to one side and the broom swung to the side as well.

"Faster!" exclaimed the hedgehog. "Faster!"

Faster and faster, higher and higher he flew in circles above the witch's cabin.

"Haha!" he cried. "Out of the way, everybody! Here comes the flying hedgehog!"

"From the sound of it, it has gotten very

windy," said the owl, sitting inside the witch's cabin, as he helped himself to another piece of magic cake.

The witch set her glass down. "I don't hear anything."

"Just listen, that whistling sound. And it seems as if I can hear somebody calling. Nothing would have happened to the hedgehog, would it?"

The witch jumped to her feet. "That hedgehog creature has taken off with my broom!" she exclaimed. "Ooyooyooy!" She stormed outside.

The owl followed her. "He's gone," he said.

"There!" shouted the witch. "There he goes. Come back!"

The hedgehog waved. "Soon!" he called out. "Tonight, maybe. Or tomorrow."

"Come back!" cried the witch, her voice cracking. "This instant!"

The hedgehog stuck out his tongue and quickly flew up higher.

The witch mumbled something. Right away the broom began to spin and zigzag.

"Don't do that!" squeaked the hedgehog. "I'm getting sick to my stomach. I'm coming, I'm coming."

The broom kept zigzagging more and more and then it dropped down, spinning. With a plop it landed in front of the cabin. The hedgehog rolled on the ground and sat up dizzily. "Everything's spinning," he said plaintively.

The witch grabbed the broom off the ground

and lashed out at the hedgehog with it. "Take that, broom thief!"

"Don't hit me!" the hedgehog cried anxiously. "I can't run away, the ground is moving."

The owl went over and stood in front of the hedgehog. "He'll never do it again," he said. "And he found your broom and honestly brought it back this morning."

The witch pushed him aside and pointed threateningly at the hedgehog. "If you take one more look at my broom, I'll turn you into a dung beetle. Then you'll be able to fly all by yourself."

The hedgehog pinched his eyes shut. "I'm not looking, I'm not looking," he cried. "See!"

The witch turned around and went inside her cabin with the broom. With a loud bang the door slammed shut behind her.

The owl looked at the door. "There's still some cake left," he said with a sigh. "But I don't think I'll go in and get any."

The hedgehog opened his eyes. "Phew, luckily the ground stopped moving. She sure was mad, wasn't she?"

"Of course she was mad," said the owl sternly. "Who would do a thing like that. You could have taken a nasty tumble."

The hedgehog hastily got up. "We'd better go, quick," he said.

When they were a safe distance from the cabin, the hedgehog asked, "Did you see how high I went?"

"Hmmm," growled the owl under his breath.

"And did you see how fast I went? Really high and really fast!"

"Hmmm."

"And I was able to do it on my first try! It really isn't very easy to fly on a broom."

"Hmmm."

The hedgehog stood still. "You haven't ever flown on a broom. I jolly well did!"

The owl looked at him with disdain. "An owl doesn't need a broom," he said.

He spread his wings and, with dignity, flew home.

THE MAGIC POTION THAT FAILED

How out of sorts the wicked witch was! She was trying to make a blue magic potion and it wasn't working. She had been cooking, sifting, and stirring for hours, but the potion kept getting browner and stank more and more.

"I just don't understand it," grumbled the witch. "It has everything in it and it still won't work."

She stirred for a little while longer, she mumbled spell after spell, but the potion didn't turn blue and the smell kept getting worse.

"It's enough to drive a person crazy!" screamed the witch. She flung her wooden spoon across the room and stomped outside, into the forest.

The blackbird saw her coming. He quickly flew into a tree and spied down on her through the leaves. He was shocked to see her turn a rabbit into a squirrel and a blueberry bush into a clump of stinging nettles.

The blackbird got out of there. As fast as he could, he flew through the entire forest, crying, "Danger! Out of the way! The wicked witch is at it again!"

The sound of running footsteps, of creaking and digging, could be heard everywhere, and then it became very quiet in the forest. Everyone had hidden.

Only the owl slowly walked down the forest path. He mumbled to himself, shook his head, and started mumbling again.

"Go home, owl!" cried the blackbird. But the owl didn't hear him, and here came the wicked witch already. Again the blackbird hid himself on a branch, behind the leaves.

The wicked witch strode closer, and suddenly all the needles on the spruce were curly and the beech tree had no leaves anymore. The witch made straight for the owl. The owl didn't even see her coming.

"Out of the way!" snapped the witch. "I'm walking here."

The owl looked up absently. "Good afternoon to you, too," he said.

"Step aside!" shouted the witch. "Or I'll turn you into a canary."

The owl nodded vaguely. "Preferably not this afternoon," he said. "But some other time, fine."

The witch stopped in her tracks and looked at him in surprise. "What did you say?"

"I'm too busy now," said the owl. "And I think it's going to rain soon."

The wicked witch took a deep breath. "Are you trying to be funny?"

"I think it's funny, too," said the owl. "It was so nice out this morning."

"Do you hear what I'm saying?" said the witch, stamping her feet. "I'm going to turn you into a canary!"

"A canary . . . ," said the owl pensively. "There aren't any here, in our forest. But there are woodpeckers and cuckoos and—"

"You're doing it on purpose! You're acting just as if you didn't understand me!"

"I don't understand it, either," the owl said helplessly. "Now, what do you really mean?"

"Grrr," said the witch. She turned on her heel. She changed a beechnut into a pine cone and gave it a good kick. Then she stomped back to her cabin.

The owl walked on, mumbling all the while.

"Wait a minute!" he heard right above his head. He looked up and saw the blackbird sitting on a branch.

"Is that you? I didn't see you," said the owl.

"I was behind the leaves," said the blackbird. "Because the wicked witch was coming."

"She's gone home again," said the owl. "She asked me something. Whether I'd come have some tea with her, I think. And she's looking for a canary."

"What is wrong with you?" the blackbird asked.

"I've been working on a poem," said the owl with a deep sigh. "All morning, already. And it just won't come out right."

The blackbird chuckled. "You really didn't hear what the witch said? She wanted to turn you into a canary."

"A ca-canary," stammered the owl. "Me? Why?"

"Because you didn't step aside."

The owl had to sit down for a minute. He fanned cool air on himself with his wing. "If I'd known that," he said disconcertedly. "How badly things might have ended . . ."

The blackbird shrugged. "But nothing happened to you, did it? Just take a look at what she did do." He pointed at the curly spruce and the bald beech tree. "We'll have to do something about that."

"A canary . . . ," sighed the owl.

"You're no help," the blackbird complained. "I'm going to get the hare. I'll be right back."

He flew away. A short while later he returned with the hare.

The hare patted the owl on the shoulder. "I hear you calmed down the wicked witch."

"Yes . . . ," said the owl, cheering up. "Well, actually, yes."

The hare looked around. "She really did go to town, didn't she."

"She also turned a rabbit into a squirrel," said the blackbird. "And blueberries into nettles."

"And me she wanted to turn into a canary," said the owl shakily.

"She'll have to turn everything back," said the hare. "And as quickly as possible. We'll go and see her."

"See her?" the owl asked fearfully.

"Yes. When her fit of anger is over, we'll be able to talk to her. Follow me."

"But—but—" said the owl. "She wanted to turn me into a—"

"Come on," said the blackbird impatiently, and he pushed the owl along behind the hare.

The door to the witch's cabin was open. The witch was grimly stirring her magic potion.

"Good afternoon," said the hare.

The witch didn't answer.

"You certainly have changed things in the forest," said the hare. "Now, could you change them all back?"

The witch turned around and pointed at the owl with her wooden spoon.

"What was with you just now? Were you trying to pull my leg, or did you really not hear what I was saying?"

"I was working on a—" the owl began.

The hare interrupted him. "He'll answer that as soon as everything has been changed back. Right, owl?"

"Uh, yes," said the owl. "I was just going to say that."

"I'm not going to change anything back," snapped the witch. "Let's have it, what was with you just now?"

The owl said nothing.

"Let's have it," the witch threatened, "or I'll turn you into a—"

"Do either of you know why she won't change anything back?" the hare whispered loudly to the others. "She can't do it. She doesn't know how to do it."

"That's what everybody is saying," the blackbird whispered back. "She isn't as good at magic

as she used to be, they say."

"Oh, no?" cried the witch. "You'll soon find out!" She waved her wooden spoon and mumbled a spell.

"She can!" exclaimed the hare, pointing outside. "Just look at the beech and the spruce. How clever!"

"Very clever," said the blackbird. "Boy, I wouldn't have believed it. And is that squirrel a rabbit again?"

"Everything is once again the way it was," said the witch. "And now I want to know why the owl was acting so strangely."

"I was working on a poem," the owl explained. "I was walking along, deep in thought about this. And the deeper in thought I am, the less I listen."

"A poem," said the witch, impressed. "Is that hard, a poem?"

"Yes," sighed the owl. "It isn't easy. Sometimes it works right away, but sometimes it doesn't work at all."

The witch nodded. "That's my problem with magic potions." She looked at the cauldron over the fire.

"Is that why you were so angry?" asked the hare.

"Yes. I want to make a blue magic potion and it just won't turn out."

"That stuff smells," said the blackbird with a disgusted look on his face. "Can't you conjure something that smells good?"

"Chocolate milk, for example," said the hare.

"Or apple pie," said the owl. "That smells very good, too."

The witch said nothing.

"But I'm sure those things are very difficult," the hare said to no one in particular. "I'm sure she can't do that."

"I can do that," said the witch. She mumbled something unintelligible and rapped on the table with her wooden spoon. Suddenly the magic potion was gone, and there on the table stood a pitcher of chocolate milk and a large apple pie.

"Ohhhhh . . . ," exclaimed the animals. They ran over to the table.

The witch sat down, too.

"How clever you are, ma'am," said the hare with his mouth full.

owl slowly flying overhead.

The blackbird quickly hid the stone under his wing. "Quiet!" he whispered. "Otherwise everybody will know that we found a precious stone."

The hedgehog looked around.

"Let's not argue," said the blackbird. "I found it—"

"I found it!"

"—but it belongs to both of us," the blackbird decided.

The hedgehog thought for a moment. "Very well, then. But I'm taking it home."

"I'm taking it home!"

They stood facing each other threateningly.

"I know," the blackbird said at last. "We won't tell anybody and we'll bury it. In a secret place."

"A secret place!" said the hedgehog. "Let's do that. But where?"

They looked all around.

"Here," said the hedgehog. "At the base of this tree."

"That won't work. There are roots there."

"Among the ferns over there."

"We'll never find it again."

"But where, then?"

"I've got it," said the blackbird. He went and stood right in front of the tree. "Twenty steps forward and ten to the side. Here!"

Together they started to dig.

When they had made a deep hole, they carefully laid the green stone on the bottom and then filled the hole back up.

"There we go," said the hedgehog as he swept some dry leaves over the secret spot. "That way you can't see it at all anymore."

"You can't tell anybody about this," said the blackbird.

"Of course not. This is our secret."

The blackbird hesitated. "Can you really keep a secret?"

"I can keep a secret very well," said the hedgehog indignantly. "Nobody will find out anything from me."

"Word of honor?"

"Word of honor!"

Solemnly they shook hands.

"Tomorrow we'll look at our stone again," said the blackbird. "I'll come over and pick you up." He was about to fly away. "You really won't tell anybody?"

"No!" shouted the hedgehog. "I won't say a thing! I never say anything!"

The blackbird quickly flew away.

Of course I can keep a secret, the hedgehog stewed.

He sprinkled a few more leaves over the secret spot and then walked off excitedly into the forest.

"A secret," he sang softly. "I know something that nobody knows! Not even the hare!"

When he had walked for a while, he could see the hare and the owl in the distance. They were leaning against a fallen tree and were talking seriously.

With a mysterious smile the hedgehog walked toward them.

I know something they jolly well don't know, he thought.

He too leaned against the tree trunk. Beaming, he looked from one to the other.

I've got a secret! he thought.

The hare looked up, annoyed. "Why are you standing there looking at us with that funny smile on your face? Is something the matter?"

"No, no, nothing," the hedgehog was quick to say. "What could be the matter?" And he started to whistle.

The hare and the owl looked at each other.

"Something is the matter," said the owl. "Why don't you tell us."

"Lalalalala . . . ," sang the hedgehog.

"Aren't we allowed to know?" asked the hare.

"No," said the hedgehog, "because it's a secret."

"A secret," said the hare, nodding. "Then you're very right not telling it."

The owl plucked at his feathers and asked uneasily, "It isn't a dangerous secret, is it? You didn't steal anything from the wicked witch or something?"

"No, of course not!" sniffed the hedgehog. "I found something."

"Oh, good," said the owl. He turned around and continued talking with the hare.

The hedgehog pulled at the hare's arm. "It's a stone," he whispered.

The hare looked up. "What's a stone?"

"What I found."

"Congratulations!" said the owl mockingly. "Now that's a find. A stone! Boyohboyohboy."

"It isn't a normal stone," said the hedgehog, insulted. "It's a green stone that glows."

"A green stone?" asked the hare.

"That glows?" asked the owl.

"Yes! But you can't tell anybody. It's a secret."

"A secret," said the owl. "So you won't tell anybody, either."

"Nobody," said the hedgehog. "Word of honor!"

The hare drummed on the tree trunk while he thought. Suddenly he said, "I don't trust this. I've never found a glowing stone in the forest. Where did you put it?"

The hedgehog looked down at the ground. "I'm not allowed to say."

"That's too bad. Then we can't go and look, either."

"It's buried near a tree, twenty steps forward and ten to the side. But I won't tell you which tree."

"Wait a minute," said the owl. "Might this be where I saw you with the blackbird when I was flying this way?"

"You guessed it!" said the hedgehog with relief. "I saw the stone first, but the blackbird picked it up and then we decided to bury it there."

"Come on," said the hare. "It's getting dark already. We'll go there right now."

A short while later they were standing at the secret spot.

The hedgehog stood in front of the tree and took twenty steps forward and ten to the side. "Here it is," he said. "But . . ."

"Somebody has already been digging here," said the owl.

The hare looked around. He ran over to the ferns and returned with the blackbird.

The hedgehog rushed at him. "You wanted to take the stone away!"

"You gave away the secret," said the blackbird.

"That isn't true! They guessed it."

"Don't argue," said the hare. "We know about it now, too, and we won't tell anybody."

"Word of honor," said the owl.

The hedgehog and the blackbird looked at each other angrily, went over to the secret spot, and together dug farther.

"There's the stone," said the hedgehog.

In the twilight it radiated a mysterious green light from the hole.

"Beautiful," said the hare. "But also a bit scary." He looked up and slapped his paw over his mouth.

The owl also looked up and fluttered backward in fright.

"What's wrong?" asked the hedgehog.

"You're glowing, too," said the hare, pale.

The hedgehog and the blackbird both glowed with a soft, green light.

"I think I already know whose stone that is," whispered the owl.

Suddenly the animals heard a whooshing sound. It was the witch, diving down on her broom. She jumped to the ground and snatched the green stone out of the hole.

"Aha!" she said. "You hid my stone!"

"He found it," squeaked the hedgehog.

"He . . . we found it," stammered the blackbird. "Here, among the leaves."

"We couldn't have known it was yours," said the hedgehog.

The witch wasn't listening. She was looking in wonder at the stone in her hand. "Beautiful," she said softly. "Especially at night."

"What's the stone for?" asked the hare.

"It's just that it's beautiful," said the witch. "You can see that, can't you?"

"Sure, sure, but isn't it a magic stone?"

The witch chuckled. "Anybody who touches the stone will glow in the dark, heeheehee. It took a lot of work to conjure that."

"But that will pass, won't it?" asked the owl nervously.

"Sadly enough, yes. After about an hour you can't see it anymore."

The animals breathed a sigh of relief.

"But if I ever lose my stone again . . . ," the witch began in a threatening tone.

"Then we'll all help you look for it!" said the hare.

"All of us!" the others exclaimed.

The witch couldn't remember what she had wanted to say. She muttered as she picked up her broom and flew away. Glowing green, she stood out against the dark sky.

"The witch is green!" exclaimed the hedgehog and the blackbird.

"Haha! The witch is glowing!"

"Hush up," said the owl. "In an hour you won't be able to see anything of it."

The hare filled in the hole.

The blackbird and the hedgehog looked at each other reproachfully.

"You wanted to take the stone away!" said the hedgehog.

"I wanted to place it in safety," said the black-

bird. "I know you can't keep a secret."

"I can, too! They guessed it."

"Don't make me laugh," said the blackbird. He pulled the owl's wing. "How were you two able to guess that here, precisely in this spot, we buried a green, glowing stone?"

"It . . . um," began the owl. "It happened like this . . ."

The hare went over and stood beside him.

"It's a secret!" he said solemnly.

THE FAIRY WITCH

 n the open place in the middle of the forest, the
hare and the hedgehog lay dozing in the sun. A
little way farther down the owl was quietly talking to himself.

The hare listened sleepily to the murmuring,
then he sat upright and asked, "Are you working
on a poem?"

"Yes," said the owl seriously. "A difficult
poem."

"What's it about?" the hedgehog asked.

"About a wise owl. A wise, old owl who gives
advice to all the animals."

"Let's hear it!" said the hedgehog.

"I still don't have very much," the owl said
shyly. "Only the beginning."

"Only the beginning, then," said the hare.

The owl cleared his throat and began:

> "A wise, old owl
> with wise, old plumes . . .

But I don't have any more yet."

"Is that all?" exclaimed the hedgehog. "Is that
why you've been sitting there all this time talking
to yourself?"

"Coming up with poems isn't easy," said the
owl, insulted. "It doesn't happen all by itself. I
don't know how it should go on."

"Do you want us to help?" asked the hare.

"I wouldn't know how. I'm trying to picture the wise owl and the animals asking for his advice. But it isn't working very well."

The hare leaped up. "We'll act it out!" he exclaimed. "Then you'll get a real picture of it."

"Do you mean," the owl said hesitantly, "I'm the wise owl and you guys . . ."

The hedgehog got up. "I'll be the wise hedgehog!" he exclaimed. "And all of you come to ask my advice."

"It's about an owl!" said the owl.

"What difference does that make! I'll be the wise, old hedgehog with wise, old spines. Come on, come and ask my advice."

"We'll take turns playing the old owl," said the hare. "He can start." He pulled the owl forward.

"Wise hedgehog," he said.

The hedgehog stamped his foot. "You have to bow down before me!"

The hare and the owl bowed. The hedgehog nodded contentedly and said in a deep voice, "Just ask. I know everything."

"We . . . um," said the owl. "We . . ."

" . . . have a question," added the hare.

"What about?" the hedgehog bellowed.

"Heeheehee," somebody snickered from behind a large tree.

"About . . . ," the owl began. He stopped and looked fearfully at the tree.

"The wicked witch!" said the hare.

"That doesn't count," said the hedgehog impatiently. "Think of something else."

"It does so count," whispered the owl. "There she is."

Chuckling, the witch came out from behind the tree.

"You're all acting so funny! What's this supposed to be?"

"A kind of play," explained the hare. "We're acting out one of the owl's poems to see how it ends."

"And I am the wise hedgehog!" exclaimed the hedgehog.

"You are?" said the witch. "You probably mean the wise-aleck hedgehog, heeheehee."

"Don't laugh!" said the hedgehog angrily. "Otherwise you can't join in."

The hare and the owl looked at each other uneasily.

"Join in?" asked the witch. "In that funny play of yours?"

"Yes," said the hedgehog. "You come to ask me for advice, too."

"I come to ask you for advice? I wouldn't dream of it! What on earth are you thinking, you windbag! I'll tie your spines in a knot, I'll . . ."

"Ma'am, you will be the good fairy," said the hare quickly.

The witch looked up. "Oh," she said, blushing.

"Stand over there," the hedgehog said, pointing. "One more step. Whoa. Yes, there."

He pushed the hare and the owl backward. "We'll start over."

The hare and the owl walked up again. "Wise hedgehog . . ."

"Bow! You have to bow!"

"Oh, yes. Wise hedgehog, we need advice. How should the owl's poem go?"

"I shall help you," said the hedgehog in a deep voice. "Go to the good fairy and everything will turn out all right."

"But I can't write poetry," whispered the witch.

"Doesn't matter," the hedgehog whispered back. "We're just pretending."

The hare and the owl bowed low before the wicked witch.

"Good day, good fairy . . ."

"Hey!" said the hare in surprise. "What beautiful flowers!"

All of a sudden the witch's hair and dress were covered with flowers.

"I just conjured them up," she said. "To look like a real fairy."

"Can I have some, too? Put some on me, too!" cried the hedgehog as he ran over to her.

Poof! Suddenly there was a little flower on each spine.

"Ohhhh . . . ," said the hedgehog. He sat down and looked proudly at his spines.

"But my poem," said the owl. "How's that going to go?"

"How does it start?" asked the witch.

"A wise, old owl
with wise, old plumes . . ."

"How clever!" said the witch admiringly. "Beautiful!"

"But it needs something else," said the owl.

"Can we add a fairy?" asked the witch. "Or a witch?"

"A fairy . . . ," said the owl thoughtfully. "Wait a minute. Don't say anything! I've got it, I've got it!"

He pinched his eyes shut and went into deep thought.

The others held their breath.

"Yes!" said the owl triumphantly. He opened his eyes and solemnly said:

"A wise, old owl
with wise, old plumes

> and the good fairy witch
> with flowers festooned
> together offer wise advice
> to hedgehogs and raccoons."

"The good fairy witch," the witch said softly. "Together offer wise advice . . . How beautiful!"

"There aren't any raccoons here!" exclaimed the hedgehog.

"But there are hedgehogs," said the hare. "One of which looks like a bouquet of flowers. Oh, no! Your flowers are gone!"

The hedgehog looked at his spines. There wasn't a flower to be seen.

"Your own fault," said the witch. "You shouldn't have been such a poor sport about that poem. It's wonderful. I'm going home right now to write it down."

She turned around and disappeared, murmuring, among the trees.

The animals watched her go.

"Her flowers are gone, too," said the hare. "Too bad."

"I do think the poem is nice, though," said the hedgehog. "And I told you that everything would turn out all right if you went to the good fairy."

"That's true," said the owl. "At times you really are a wise hedgehog."

The hedgehog nodded.

"Only sometimes," said the hare softly.

The hare was standing outside his door, looking thoughtfully at the ground. "Strange," he muttered.

"Hare!" he heard. He looked up. The hedgehog was limping down the forest path.

"What happened to you?" the hare asked. "Did you fall down?"

"I sprained my foot," the hedgehog complained. "All of a sudden there was this deep hole in the path and I stepped in it."

"There's a deep hole here, too," said the hare. "Here, right outside my door. I just discovered it."

"There's another one," the hedgehog said, pointing. "Over there by that bush."

"I don't get it," said the hare. "Who'd go around digging holes?"

The owl flew up hurriedly. "Hare," he said in a rush. "I have to talk to you. There's something strange going on."

"What is it?"

"I was just leaving my house," said the owl, "and you'll never guess what I saw, in front of my tree."

"A hole?" inquired the hedgehog.

"Three holes," said the owl.

"Three?" exclaimed the hare. "Do you mean holes like this?"

"Yes!" said the owl. "Only deeper."

"The hole in the forest path is even deeper," said the hedgehog. "I sprained my foot in it. Look, I almost can't walk anymore."

"In the path, too," said the owl nervously. "This is very unusual, this isn't as it should be, this . . ."

The hare nodded pensively. "It's very strange. Who could have done that?"

"The wicked witch, of course!" cried the hedgehog. "Who else?"

The hare shook his head. "I don't think so. This isn't something the wicked witch would do."

"It isn't?" said the hedgehog. "Once she tied my spines in knots, so you know you can expect anything."

"No," said the hare. "Magic tricks and potions, sure, but digging holes? No. She wouldn't do that."

"This is very unusual," whispered the owl. "Maybe there's a big diggerbeetle or a hole epidemic or . . ."

"Come on," said the hare. "Let's go over to the witch's and see. Maybe there are holes in the ground over there, too."

"Or she's just in the process of digging them," stewed the hedgehog. He walked along with the others.

"How's your foot?" asked the owl.

"My foot?" the hedgehog asked in surprise. "Oh, my foot! It's already getting a little better." And he started limping again.

"Look!" exclaimed the hare. "There's another one."

"And over there on that side, too," the owl said, afraid. "There are more and more. Maybe it's an illness, a contagious forest illness."

When they arrived at the wicked witch's little cabin in the forest, the witch was near her front door with an annoyed look on her face, digging.

"Aha!" exclaimed the hedgehog. "You see? She did it!"

"That shovel is much too big," said the hare. "It's impossible. I think she's filling a hole back in."

The witch looked threateningly at the animals. "Did you dig holes outside my door?" she asked.

"No," said the hare. "That's exactly why we came. I've got a hole outside my door, too."

"I have three," said the owl.

"I have four," said the witch, furious.

"And I sprained my foot in one," the hedgehog reported. "A hole just like that one next to the rain barrel."

"Five!" said the witch, throwing her shovel down.

"This is very unusual," said the owl in a shaky voice. "This is scary. Brrr . . ."

"If I catch them . . . ," muttered the witch.

The hare went over to her. "We'll protect you!" he said.

The witch looked at him in surprise. "From what?"

"From the hole digger," the owl explained. "It could be a big diggerbeetle or a digging monster."

"I didn't see any monsters," said the witch

brusquely. "And if I see any, it won't be all fun and games for them. Ooyooyooy."

"We'll go and investigate," said the hare. "Ma'am, you will fly on your broom over this side of the forest. Owl, you will fly over that side. In the meantime I will run through the entire forest. That way we ought to be able to discover what's going on."

"And me?" inquired the hedgehog. "Where should I look?"

"You're staying here. You sprained your foot."

"It's better already! I want to go, too! I want to catch the hole diggers!"

"Good. Then you go to the sand-drift."

"The sand-drift!" said the hedgehog with disdain. "What goes on over there? Nothing ever happens there. Can't I run with you?"

The hare winked at the witch and the owl. "The sand-drift happens to be very important," he said. "There's room there to dig."

The hedgehog smiled proudly. "I'm going to catch them!" he exclaimed. "Watch out, hole diggers! Here comes the hedgehog!" and he marched off.

"As long as a hedgehog has his spines
there is nothing for him to fear,"

sang the hedgehog as loudly as he could. On the way he saw several more holes. I'll have to remember that, he thought. The hare should know about them.

He kept up a good pace until he reached the sand-drift. When he got there, he stood still and looked over the entire stretch of sand.

"Is anybody here?" called the hedgehog.

Silence.

"This is the hedgehog speaking! Hole diggers, give yourselves up!"

Still no response.

Hesitantly the hedgehog walked farther. "Whoa! A hole! You see? Here, too."

The hedgehog heard something. It seemed as if there was whispering going on somewhere . . . Fearfully the hedgehog looked around. There was no one to be seen, and yet he heard whispers and digging.

"Mercy!" squeaked the hedgehog. He turned around and began running back to the forest. Now he could hear giggling and choked laughter.

The hedgehog stood still and looked back over his shoulder. "Hey . . . ," he said under his breath. Twelve ears were sticking out from behind a low

dune.

The hedgehog tiptoed over to the dune and looked behind it. There were six young rabbits giggling and horsing around digging holes.

"Aha!" exclaimed the hedgehog. "You're the hole diggers!"

The young rabbits squealed and pelted him with sand. "Yes! We're digging everywhere! Everywhere in the forest we're digging holes! In turns!"

"Why?" asked the hedgehog.

"Just because! No reason! For fun! Whoever digs the deepest hole!"

"But that's dangerous!" said the hedgehog. "Somebody can fall in and sprain his foot!"

The young rabbits looked at one another in dismay. Then they all began to hop again, shouting, "Then we'll think of something else! Who's going to think of something else? Whoever thinks of something else first!"

"First you're all coming with me to see the hare," said the hedgehog sternly. "To tell him that you dug all those holes."

"And get yelled at, right? No way! You go!" the young rabbits shouted. And off they went, hopping and shoving one another, to the other side of the sand-drift.

The hedgehog watched them go. Then he looked at the holes.

"I solved the riddle," he said proudly. "I know who the hole diggers are. Quick, I have to go tell the others."

He ran back to the wicked witch's little cabin.

When he arrived the witch was just landing by the door.

"Witch!" the hedgehog called, out of breath. "I know who did it! I found the hole diggers!"

The witch leaned her broom against the side of the house. "Shut up," she said moodily. "Three times I flew over the forest, I looked everywhere and there's nothing to be seen. Nothing!"

"But I found them," said the hedgehog. "They're—"

"There's the owl," said the witch. "Maybe he discovered something."

The owl flew down.

"And?" asked the witch.

The owl shook his head. "I saw a few more holes," he said, "but that's all. The digging monster has hidden itself well."

"It isn't a monster!" exclaimed the hedgehog. "It's the—"

The hare came running up. "Did any of you find anything?" he asked.

"Nothing," said the witch.

"Only holes," said the owl.

"I—" the hedgehog began.

"I looked through the entire forest," said the hare. "I went everywhere. I discovered a couple of new holes, but no trace of whoever did it."

The hedgehog tugged at his arm. "But listen! I know who . . ."

The hare pushed him away. "Not now. We'll

listen to you in a little while, but right now we're busy."

"So don't!" said the hedgehog furiously. He sat on the ground, sulking.

"What should we do?" asked the owl.

"I have a plan," said the hare importantly. "We'll warn all the animals and we'll take turns guarding the holes. I'll ask the birds to pay close attention and tell me right away about any new holes. Then we'll have to find out who's doing it."

"And then it won't be all fun and games for them," said the witch sourly.

The owl plucked at his feathers and whispered, "Maybe they're invisible digging monsters. Maybe we'll never find out who—"

"If nobody wants to listen, then no, you won't," said the hedgehog testily.

"Listen to whom?" asked the witch.

"To me!" said the hedgehog. He took a deep breath.

"I found the hole diggers," he said quickly. "It's the young rabbits. And they aren't digging any more holes because I explained to them how dangerous it is. And now I'm going to put a bandage around my foot. See you later." He got up and limped off.

A heavy silence fell.

The hare cleared his throat.

The witch stared at her shoes.

"The young rabbits," the owl said with relief. "Of course. I suspected that the whole time."

"Those little brats," said the witch. "I'll get them!"

"Don't bother," said the hare quickly. "I have a better idea. We . . . um . . . we should really bake a cake for the hedgehog. What do you all think about a big cake with fruit?"

"A cake with nuts," said the owl.

"A cake with holes, heeheehee," chuckled the witch.

"That's what we'll do!" said the hare. "A big cake with fruit and nuts and holes."

The hedgehog came running back, beaming. "Not too many holes!" he exclaimed.

A QUIET EVENING

It was a hot day. The heat hung heavily among the trees. Even in the shade it was hot.

Early in the evening the hedgehog was trudging through the forest on his way to the pond. Maybe it would be a little cooler near the water.

When he reached the pond, he noticed that somebody else was already there.

The hare was sitting at the edge with his feet in the water. He waved at the hedgehog. "Come on! It's delicious here."

The hedgehog came and sat beside him and also stuck his feet in the water.

"Ahhh. I should have thought of that sooner."

"I did think of it sooner," said the hare with satisfaction. "I've been sitting here for a while already." He picked up a pebble and made it skip across the water. "Can you do that?"

"Yes," said the hedgehog and he closed his eyes. "But in a bit, when I've cooled off."

The hare skipped another stone across the water.

"Don't make so much noise," said the hedgehog.

"I'm not making any noise. You almost can't hear this."

The hedgehog opened his eyes. "Where's that splashing sound coming from, then?"

"From behind those tall rushes over there.

Maybe somebody's swimming."

The splashing sound came closer.

Curious, the hare and the hedgehog looked at the rushes. Suddenly they saw a hat appear, and there was the wicked witch.

She was holding up her skirt a little and slowly wading through the water, close to the edge of the pond.

"She's wading," whispered the hare.

"Bah," the hedgehog muttered under his breath. "Just when I'm sitting quietly, she has to come along."

"What difference does that make? There's plenty of space, isn't there?"

"Sure. But soon enough she'll want to cast spells on us."

"She won't," said the hare. "It's way too hot to cast spells."

The witch approached with splashing steps.

"Hello there," the hare called. "The water's nice, isn't it?"

The hedgehog choked back a giggle.

The witch fixed him with a look. "What's there to laugh about?"

The hedgehog pointed. "Your skirt's hanging in the water."

Vexed, the witch pulled the hem of her skirt up. "That's no laughing matter," she snapped.

"Is too!" giggled the hedgehog. "Because now the back of your skirt's hanging in the water."

"Stop it!" threatened the witch.

"I'm allowed to laugh, aren't I?"

"But not at me," said the witch. "Stop it or I'll turn you into a stickleback."

"No!" cried the hedgehog, and he spattered water at the witch with his feet.

The witch took a step backward. But the pond was a lot deeper there. She lost her balance and disappeared underwater.

Startled, the hedgehog and the hare jumped to their feet.

The witch came up again, coughing and spluttering, and started to swim to the side. She had an angry look on her face.

The hedgehog wanted to run away, but the hare held him back. "You, stay here. Maybe she needs help."

"But she's going to turn me into a stickleback," whimpered the hedgehog. "She's furious! Just look."

The hare looked nervously at the wicked witch who was swimming closer with powerful strokes. "The water's nice, isn't it?" he called out uncertainly.

The witch looked up. "Yes!" she said in surprise. She let herself float. Then she started swimming in circles, splashing all the while.

"Swimming is the best thing you can do when it's this hot," said the hare.

"It cools you off nicely," said the hedgehog.

The witch dived down once more before she swam to the side.

"That was delicious," she said and stepped out of the water.

Dripping, she stood on the edge.

The hedgehog choked back his laughter with his paw.

The witch looked at him sternly. "Are you going to start again?"

"You look just like a waterfall," giggled the hedgehog.

"Now, that's enough!" shrieked the witch. "It's your fault that I'm so wet. And a witch doesn't let herself be ridiculed!" She walked threateningly toward the hedgehog.

The hedgehog took a step backward. And another step and another one and—sploosh!—he stepped backward into the water.

The witch burst out laughing. "The water's nice, isn't it?" she howled.

The hare ran forward and helped the hedgehog to the side.

Dripping, the hedgehog stood beside the witch. "Don't laugh!" he said indignantly.

"Come sit down for a moment and relax," said the hare. "With this weather, you'll both be dry again in no time."

A moment later they were sitting beside one another at the water's edge.

The hare picked up a stone. "Ma'am, can you do this?" he asked and skipped a stone across the water.

The witch gave it a try. Her stone immediately sank into the pond.

"You have to take a flat stone," said the hedgehog. "And then throw it fast. Look, like this."

The witch tried it again. "That time was better," she said proudly. "Now you again."

The hare watched the stones dreamily. "What a quiet evening," he said.

"Yes," said the witch. "It's really much too hot to do any magic."

"And much too hot to run away," said the hedgehog, and he stuck his feet in the water.

THE TREE SONG

One evening the hare and the blackbird were taking a walk.

"Do you have any idea what's wrong with the owl?" asked the hare. "He's been so gloomy the last few days."

"He's never what you'd call cheerful, though," said the blackbird.

"No, but I've never seen him as gloomy as he is now."

"I have an idea," said the blackbird importantly. "In my opinion, he's worried about something. And that's why . . ."

"Shhh," whispered the hare. "There he is." He pointed at a beech tree.

The owl was sitting on a low branch, glumly mumbling to himself, "Oh, the trees in the wood . . ."

He thought long and hard, sighed, and began again, "Oh, the trees . . ."

"What's wrong with the trees?" asked the blackbird.

The owl gave a start and looked down. "I didn't see you two coming. I'm working on a poem, but it isn't really coming along."

"But what's wrong with the trees?" asked the blackbird again.

"Nothing," said the owl shyly. "That's the first line of my poem. It's supposed to be very beauti-

ful and mournful, but I'm really not very good at poetry."

"I'm sure it isn't as bad as all that," said the hare. "Let's hear it."

The owl cleared his throat and began reciting solemnly:

> "Oh, the trees in the wood
> how very long they've stood."

The hare and the blackbird looked at each other.

"But there are young trees, too," said the hare.

"And bushes," said the blackbird.

The owl nodded sadly. "I told you it wasn't working."

The hare bit his lip. "It sounds very nice," he said quickly. "How does the rest of it go?"

"Oh, in this wood the trees
let go of all their leaves."

"Pretty obvious," said the blackbird. "They always do that in the fall."

The hare gave him a nudge.

"Oh, the trees around our home
may feel they're all alone."

The owl fell silent and looked uncertainly at the hare.

"It's beautiful," said the hare. "Beautiful and mournful."

"Give me a cheerful poem," said the blackbird. "Can't you make up a cheerful poem?"

"Only when I'm cheerful," said the owl with a sigh. "And I'm not cheerful."

"What's wrong, then?"

The owl shifted back and forth on the branch and said, "I've discovered that I'm not a poet. My poems aren't beautiful."

The hare wanted to say something, but he didn't know what.

"I've always wanted to be a poet," said the owl, his head bent down, "and I'm not. I think I'll go home." He spread his wings and slowly flew away.

The hare watched him go. "What idiots we are," he said.

"Idiots?" asked the blackbird, insulted.

"Yes. He was sad already, and now he's even sadder because we made comments about his poem."

"Oh, dear," said the blackbird. "But I was right. I told you he was worried about something."

The hare sat down. "We have to help him. Otherwise he'll never dare to make up more poems. And he enjoys doing that so much."

"I'd like to help," said the blackbird, "but I really can't rhyme. I can sing but not rhyme."

The hare drummed on the ground and gazed thoughtfully into the distance.

Suddenly he jumped up. "Sing!" he said. "That's it! Can you think of a nice melody to go with that tree poem?"

"A nice, mournful melody?" asked the blackbird. "A tree song?"

"Yes! Then we'll go sing it for the owl and he can hear for himself how beautiful his poem is."

"It isn't that beautiful," muttered the blackbird.

"If we sing it, it will be," said the hare.

The following evening the hare ran to the tree where the owl lived. The owl sat hunched up by the door.

"How's your poem coming along?" asked the hare.

The owl shook his head. "I'm not going to make up any more poems. Never again. I can't do it anyway."

"You can, too," said the hare.

The owl said nothing.

"We have a surprise for you," said the hare mysteriously.

"Not necessary," muttered the owl to himself. "Don't bother."

The hare turned around and waved.

The blackbird came out from behind a tree and whistled shrilly, and from all sides animals came to the owl's tree: the hedgehog, the squirrel, the bat, lots of rabbits, and even more birds . . .

"Ready?" cried the hare. "One, two, three!"

The animals began to sing:

> "Oh, the trees in the wood
> how very long they've stood.
> Oh, in this wood the trees
> let go of all their leaves.
> Oh, the trees around our home
> may feel they're all alone . . ."

It sounded a little out of key here and there because some of the animals couldn't hold a tune, but the birds sang so loudly that it couldn't really be noticed.

When it was over, the hare asked, "Well? What do you think of it?"

The owl was speechless for a moment. Then he said hoarsely, "Lovely, lovely. I never thought my poem could sound so beautiful . . ."

"It is a beautiful melody, at that," said the blackbird.

"And it was sung very beautifully," exclaimed the hedgehog.

"Yes, of course," said the hare, "but without the owl's poem, there wouldn't have been a song."

"That's true," exclaimed the animals. "Long live the owl! Long live our poet!"

All of a sudden the owl was so happy that he couldn't sit still anymore. He fluttered up and down, saying with awe, "I'm a poet! I really am—"

"Ooyooyooy!"

"—a poet," the owl squeaked, and looked to the side fearfully.

The wicked witch was standing in the bushes.

"What's going on here?" she croaked.

"Nothing, nothing at all," stammered the hare. "We're just singing a song."

"A song . . ." The witch looked suspiciously from one animal to the next. "A song about me, no doubt!"

"No, no, not at all, honestly, we wouldn't dare!" all the animals cried out at once.

"I don't believe a word of it," said the witch. She shuffled forward and sat down in front of the owl's tree. "Let's hear that song, then. And if it's about me, I'll turn you all into stinkhorns."

"One, two, three," counted the hare, and they all sang again:

"Oh, the trees in the wood . . ."

The witch grew pale. She blinked her eyes.

"Oh, the trees around our home
may feel they're all alone . . ."

The last tones faded away. It was quiet for a moment. Then there was a loud sniffing sound.

The animals nudged one another and pointed at the witch.

"Boohoohoo!" sobbed the witch. "Boohoohoo!"

The hare walked over to her and patted her on the shoulder. "Now, now, now," he said shyly.

The witch blew her nose, heaved a sigh, and whispered, "How beautiful, it's so beautiful."

She looked up. The animals stood around her bashfully. The witch began to chuckle.

"Heeheehee, what are you standing there for, looking stupid! Heeheehee."

"We think it's a pity that you have to cry," said the hedgehog.

"I always cry when I hear a sad song. That isn't a pity, it's great."

"How strange!" said the hedgehog.

"That isn't strange," said the owl. "I always feel that way, too."

The witch nodded in agreement. "I love sad songs," she said. "The sadder, the better."

"I'll think up another poem," promised the owl.

"Even sadder?"

"Much, much sadder, even!"

The witch smiled happily.

"Will you think up a cheerful poem for me?" asked the blackbird.

"Yes!" said the owl, beaming. "I'm feeling cheerful again, so now it'll work."

THE WICKED WITCH BAKES COOKIES

There was a sweet smell around the witch's cabin. The wicked witch was baking cookies. A big plate of them was already cooling off by the open window.

"Baking is really a kind of magic, too," said the witch contentedly.

Outside there was a crunching sound.

"What's that sound I keep hearing?" murmured the witch. She looked at the window. "Hey! That plate was full, wasn't it?"

On the plate by the window there now lay only a couple of cookies.

There was more crunching outside.

The witch went over to look, but she saw no one. She hid behind the curtain and peered outside.

The hedgehog came tiptoeing up. He snatched a cookie from the plate and disappeared, munching, behind a tree.

"Just what I thought," muttered the witch. "But he'll be sorry. Ooyooyooy."

She went over to the cupboard, took a spoonful of white powder out of a canister, and sprinkled it over the biggest cookie.

"Looks like powdered sugar, heeheehee," she chuckled.

She stood behind the curtain again.

There was the hedgehog again. He quickly took the biggest cookie and walked off.

The witch flung open the door. "Taste good?" she called out.

The hedgehog cringed. He looked around, ready to run away. But the witch just stood in the doorway.

"Delicious," said the hedgehog. "Very delicious. Except that last one tasted a little salty."

"That wasn't salt," the witch said with a chuckle. "Would you like another one? Come and get it, heeheehee."

The hedgehog looked at her uncertainly.

"Come on," said the witch. "There are lots more inside."

The hedgehog took a step forward. He was shocked to discover that he wasn't going forward at all, but backward.

"Whoa," said the hedgehog.

He took another step forward and again he went backward.

"How can that be?" he asked, bewildered.

The witch burst out laughing. "You'll have to walk backward from now on, my dear little hedgehog!" she howled. "A little inconvenient, but you'll get used to it."

"Hey!" shouted the hedgehog. "That's mean! Make me go forward again!"

"I wouldn't dream of it," said the witch. "Shouldn't have stolen any cookies." She went inside and slammed the door shut.

"They weren't even good!" exclaimed the hedgehog angrily. "They were rotten! Yuck!"

From the witch's cabin, there was only silence.

The hedgehog sighed. He tried to walk forward. At each step he went backward.

"What now?" said the hedgehog, thinking hard. "To the hare! Sometimes he has good ideas."

He looked over his shoulder and carefully started backing down the forest path. At first it went all right. But when he started walking faster, he tripped over a branch, bumped into a tree, fell into a dip . . .

"I won't get anywhere this way," he grumbled. "I'll just have to try something else." He rolled himself up into a ball and shoved off gently, and there he was, rolling backward through the forest. Slowly at first, but soon he was going faster. He bumped right through dips, he bounced over branches and stones. The animals he met along the way quickly leaped to the side. The hedgehog didn't even notice. He rolled on, faster and faster.

The hare was standing outside his house, talking with the owl. Suddenly he saw something strange on the forest path. "Just look at that!" he said, surprised.

The owl looked around.

A prickly ball was rolling at full speed along the path. At the end of the path it rolled into a deep pit. A moment later the hedgehog carefully scrambled backward out of the pit. He looked over his shoulder and walked backward toward the hare and the owl.

"What are you doing?" asked the hare. "Is that a game?"

The hedgehog sat down and looked up indignantly.

"You don't honestly think I'm doing this for the fun of it?"

"Why are you, then?"

"I can't walk forward anymore," squeaked the hedgehog. "By accident I picked up one of the

witch's cookies, just one cookie, and then she bewitched me backward."

"Just one cookie?" inquired the owl.

The hedgehog looked at the ground. "Well, okay, a couple more. They smelled so good."

"But for a couple of cookies she won't have you walking backward forever?"

"She will!" lamented the hedgehog. "She said so."

"Just try walking normally," said the hare.

"Maybe it's over already."

The hedgehog got up and took a couple of steps. "You see. Backward."

The hare thought long and hard. "And if you try walking backward?" he asked. "Maybe then you'll go forward."

The hedgehog stepped backward. He shook his head. "Backward, too," he said and with a sigh he sat down again.

"Maybe you'll get used to it," the owl said comfortingly.

The hedgehog looked at him, furious.

"Come on, owl," said the hare. "We'll go see the witch."

"See the witch!" said the owl, startled.

"Yes. We'll go and ask her if she won't hex the hedgehog forward again."

"She won't do it anyway," the hedgehog sniffed. "Once she tied my spines in knots and now this . . . She always has to pick on me."

"We're going to try anyway," said the hare. "Are you coming, owl?"

The owl coughed. "Wouldn't it be better if I stayed with the hedgehog?"

The hare shrugged. "If you don't dare, I'll go by myself."

"I do so dare," said the owl. "Of course I dare." He heaved a sigh and followed the hare.

"Mmm, it smells delicious here," said the hare when they were near the wicked witch's cabin.

"Just remember not to eat anything inside," said the owl nervously. "You know what'll happen then."

The hare knocked.

"Come in!" the witch called out.

The hare and the owl pushed the door open and went in. The witch was sitting at the table drinking tea and eating cookies.

"Look what we have here. Company!" she said. "Would either of you like a cookie?"

"No, no! Thank you!" the hare and the owl exclaimed at once.

"They turned out very well," the witch said, insulted.

"Yes, but . . . ," said the owl.

"The hedgehog . . . ," said the hare.

The witch started chuckling. "The hedgehog stole a cookie with backward powder on it. But these have no powder on them." She slid the plate toward them.

The hare hesitated. But the cookies smelled so delicious that he took one anyway. The owl plucked nervously at his feathers.

"Mmm, delicious," said the hare. He looked at his feet and took a step forward. It worked! Relieved, he took another cookie.

Now the owl also dared.

"We're coming about the hedgehog," said the hare. "He's so sorry."

"Terribly sorry," said the owl.

The witch ate a cookie.

"He's black and blue," said the hare, "because he bumps into everything. It's nasty walking backward."

"Very nasty," said the owl.

The witch ate another cookie.

"He's rolling backward through the forest," said the hare. "And that's dangerous for the other animals."

"Very dangerous," said the owl.

"He's rolling?" exclaimed the witch. "Backward? That I have to see!"

"He's sitting in front of my house," said the hare. "If you would just walk over with us . . ."

The witch shook her head. "I'll have him come here." She mumbled something.

The hare and the owl waited uneasily.

After a while they heard crunching and bonking. Through the open door they could see the hedgehog rolling toward the cabin. At full speed he rolled inside.

The witch slapped the table, she was laughing so hard. "Heehahoo! That looks so funny! Heehahoo!"

The hedgehog rolled at full speed into her feet.

"Ow!" yelled the witch. "That pricks!" and she clutched her foot.

"That's what I mean," said the hare. "It's dangerous for everyone if the hedgehog is rolling that way through the forest."

"Very dangerous," said the owl.

"Come out, you," commanded the witch.

The hedgehog stood up.

"First you steal cookies and then you prick me in my foot!"

"I can't help it," squeaked the hedgehog. "I rolled here without doing anything."

"That's true," said the hare. "You used magic to get him here, ma'am."

"And those cookies." said the hedgehog, "They smelled so delicious that I just had to taste one."

"One?" the witch asked threateningly.

"At first," said the hedgehog quickly. "But that one was so delicious that I had to take more."

"That's true, too," said the hare. "These are the most delicious cookies I've ever tasted."

"Absolutely the most delicious," the owl said and he looked longingly at the plate.

The hare cleared his throat and said solemnly, "Our witch bakes the best cookies in the whole forest!" He jabbed the owl.

"In the whole world!" the owl said quickly.

The witch flushed red with pride. "Then have another one," she said.

The hedgehog took a step forward.

"Not you!" cried the witch. "You've already had enough."

The hare and the owl danced up and down. "Yippee, yippee!"

Indignantly the hedgehog looked around. "How mean! Cheering because I can't have any. Bah!"

"That's not why we're cheering," said the hare.

"You were walking forward!"

"Forward!" exclaimed the hedgehog. He took a giant step. Then he ran around the table. "I can walk forward again! Yippee, yippee, yippee!"

The witch pointed at him. "Now go home. And remember, don't ever snatch anything again."

"Never again," promised the hedgehog.

The hare and the owl each took a cookie. "Thank you! When you decide to bake some more, we'll come over and help."

They went outside. The hedgehog skipped after them. In the doorway, he turned around.

"Witch," he wheedled, "dear witch, may I have a cookie, for the road?"

The witch slowly got up.

The hedgehog backed away.

The witch picked up a cookie and looked as if she was going to stick it in her mouth. Suddenly she smiled. "Catch!" she called as she tossed the cookie outside.

THE HEDGEHOG GETS SICK

One morning the hare ran to the hedgehog's house and drummed on the door with his fists. There was no answer.

The hare opened the door and looked inside. The hedgehog was sitting in a chair with a blanket around his shoulders.

"Didn't you hear me?" asked the hare as he stepped inside.

"Yes . . . ," said the hedgehog.

"What's wrong, why are you wrapped in that blanket?"

"It's so cold," the hedgehog complained.

"Cold? It isn't cold at all, it's wonderful weather. Do you want to go on a picnic? The owl's coming, too."

"Eheh eheh eheh," coughed the hedgehog.

"What did you say?"

"I didn't say anything, I was coughing."

The hare studied the hedgehog. He was taken aback. "You look funny. Are you sick?"

The hedgehog shivered.

"You've got a fever!" said the hare. "You should be in bed."

"I don't want to go to bed. I want to go on a picnic."

"You don't think we're going on a picnic if you're sick? We'll wait and do that when you're better again."

"Then I'll go to bed," said the hedgehog. With difficulty he got up, went over to his bed, and crawled under the blankets.

"Would you like something to drink?" asked the hare.

The hedgehog shook his head.

"Something to eat?"

"No . . ."

"Something to read?"

"No . . . ," whispered the hedgehog and he closed his eyes.

The hare walked back and forth nervously. "How do you feel?"

"Hurt," said the hedgehog hoarsely. "Hurt all over."

There was a knock at the door and the owl came in with a big picnic basket. "Look!" he exclaimed proudly. "Full of delicious things."

"Shhh," shushed the hare, pointing at the

hedgehog.

The owl started. "Is he sick?"

"Yes," said the hare. "He has a fever."

"And pain," said the hedgehog plaintively.

The owl set the basket down in a corner. "I'll stay here," he said.

"I'll stay, too," said the hare.

Together they took care of the hedgehog. They gave him things to drink, they made tea and dry toast, the hare read aloud from the hedgehog's favorite book, the owl recited poems . . . And after all that, they just sat quietly at his bedside, because the hedgehog kept getting sicker. He lay very still, with his eyes closed. He didn't want to eat anything and didn't respond anymore, either.

The hare and the owl became more and more uneasy.

"What should we do?" asked the owl.

The hare sat with his head in his paws at the foot of the bed. Suddenly he stood up. "I'm going to get the witch," he said.

"The witch . . . ," said the owl. "Do you think she . . ."

"Yes," said the hare. "She knows everything about herbs, and she must know at least a hundred magic spells. Maybe she can make the hedgehog better."

The owl looked at the hedgehog and nodded. "Go quickly, then," he said.

The hare tiptoed outside and ran to the wicked witch's cabin. He pounded on the door. The witch opened it.

"Don't disturb me," she said. "I'm busy."

"It's urgent," said the hare, out of breath. "The hedgehog is sick."

"The hedgehog," said the witch with disdain. "The hedgehog is always exaggerating."

"This time he isn't, really," said the hare. "He has a high fever and pain everywhere. Don't you have something to make him better?"

"He'll get better by himself," said the witch. She shuffled over to the cupboard and took a little bottle off the top shelf.

"He doesn't want to eat anything," said the hare. "And he won't say anything anymore. He just lies there."

The witch took a small box out of a drawer.

"Please, won't you come take a look at him, ma'am?" asked the hare. "Please. We're so worried."

"I'm sure it isn't all that bad," said the witch.

"No, no," cried the hare in desperation. "He's really—"

The witch took her broom and shoved the hare aside. "Out of the way! I've got other things to do." She went outside and leaped on her broom, and away she went.

The hare heaved a sigh. "Miserable woman! She wouldn't even listen!"

He looked at the cupboard. So many bottles! Wouldn't there be a medicine for the hedgehog among them?

The hare stood on his tiptoes and took a little bottle off a shelf. There was a green, cloudy potion in it. The hare sniffed at it. Phew! Quickly he put the bottle back.

On the bottom shelf there was a saucer of yellow powder. That smelled better. "Let's just see what happens," said the hare softly.

He picked up the saucer and shook a little bit of powder on the table. There was a loud boom and suddenly the tablecloth was yellow.

With shaking paws the hare put the saucer back in the cupboard.

"Don't touch!" he said to himself. "Imagine if I turned the hedgehog into something scary or make him completely vanish . . ."

He shivered at the thought. Quickly he went outside. On his way he picked flowers for the hedgehog.

When the hare reached the hedgehog's house, he saw that there was a broom beside the door.

"Hey!" said the hare. He went in quickly.

The hedgehog still lay quietly in bed. The witch sat beside him mumbling magic spells, and the owl was carrying over a glass of water.

"You came anyway!" exclaimed the hare to the witch. "I thought . . ."

The witch looked around. "There you are, finally! What took you so long?"

The hare found a vase. "I was picking flowers," he said. "And . . . and . . . your tablecloth's a bit yellow, by accident . . ."

"What?" exclaimed the witch. "Were you nosing around in my cupboard?"

"I—I was looking for a medicine for the hedgehog . . . ," said the hare, stumbling over his words.

The witch chuckled. "It isn't in the cupboard anymore, because I've got it with me."

She pulled a little bottle out of her apron and emptied it into the glass of water.

"Drink this," she said to the hedgehog.

"No," whispered the hedgehog. "Then I'll turn into a pine cone or a fruit fly."

"Drink it," threatened the witch, "or I will turn you into a fruit fly."

The hedgehog clenched his teeth.

"Come on, drink it," said the owl. "She means well."

"Even one sip helps," said the witch.

Reluctantly the hedgehog took a tiny sip.

"Delicious!" he said, surprised, and emptied the glass in a single gulp.

"I thought so," said the witch and she took out a small box. "Now a little powder."

The hedgehog gulped it down.

"Yuck!" he exclaimed. "Yuck, that tastes rotten!"

"Heeheehee, but it does help," chuckled the witch.

"Another bite?"

The hedgehog shook his head and closed his eyes.

"How do you feel now?" inquired the hare.

"Bad," said the hedgehog weakly. "It hurts all over. My head . . . my toes . . . zzzz."

"What happened to him?" the owl asked anxiously.

"He's sleeping," said the witch. "And now, to work, you two. Make food. Lots of delicious food."

The owl lifted the picnic basket and set it on the table. "Here's a basket already filled with delicious things."

The hare opened the cupboard. "And here's a lot more."

The witch took out a couple of pans and together the three of them prepared a huge meal. Everything the hedgehog liked, they made.

When it was all spread out on the table, the witch slammed two pot lids together. "Wake up, sleepy head!" she cried.

The hedgehog opened his eyes and yawned loudly.

"How do you feel now?" asked the hare.

"Pain . . . ," said the hedgehog. "In my stomach."

The owl looked worriedly at the witch. She picked up a spoon and said, "You have to eat something."

"I can't eat," said the hedgehog. "I've got a stomach ache."

The witch shrugged. "Then we'll eat."

"I'm not very hungry," said the hare.

"Me neither," said the owl.

"But I am!" said the witch and she filled the plates.

The hedgehog sniffed. "Maybe I should try a bite," he said weakly.

"Good!" exclaimed the hare. "What would you like?"

The hedgehog looked at the table. "Everything!" he said.

"But you've got a stomach ache," said the owl.

The hedgehog said nothing for a long time. He ate and he ate and he ate until the table was almost empty. Then he leaned back and panted, "That wasn't a stomach ache. That was hunger!"

"Hurrah! You're better again!" exclaimed the hare and the owl.

The witch got up. "I told you he'd get better by himself."

"Not all by himself," said the hare. "You helped."

The owl nodded.

The hedgehog grasped the witch's hand. "You're the best witch in the world."

"Sure, sure," said the witch shyly. "Out of the way, all of you. I have other things to do today." She went outside, picked up her broom, and disappeared.

The hedgehog looked at the open door. "What beautiful weather! I want to go outside."

"We can't go on a picnic anymore," said the owl. "Everything's been eaten."

"We can go pick flowers," said the hare.

The hedgehog pointed at the vase. "I've already got flowers."

"Flowers for the witch!" said the hare.

Hanna Kraan teaches Italian and works as an interpreter. *Tales of the Wicked Witch* (Puffin) was her first book for children, and she has written four more collections of stories about these much-loved characters. *The Wicked Witch Is at It Again* is the second volume to be published in the United States. A thirteen-part television series based on the Wicked Witch stories has been shown on Dutch television and another series is in production.

Hanna Kraan lives in the Netherlands.